To all the mighty teachers and students
who have welcomed me into their
schools and libraries. —DL

To all my friends, young and old. —LC

Dial Books for Young Readers
An imprint of Penguin Random House LLC, New York

First published in the United States of America by Dial Books for Young Readers,
an imprint of Penguin Random House LLC, 2023

Visit us online at penguinrandomhouse.com.

Library of Congress Cataloging-in-Publication Data is available.

Manufactured in China • 9780525555445 • 10 9 8 7 6 5 4 3 2 1
TOPL

Design by Mina Chung & Lily Malcom • Text set in Biko

The publisher does not have any control over and does not assume any
responsibility for author or third-party websites or their content.

The art for this book was created using acrylic paint
and color pencils on watercolor paper.

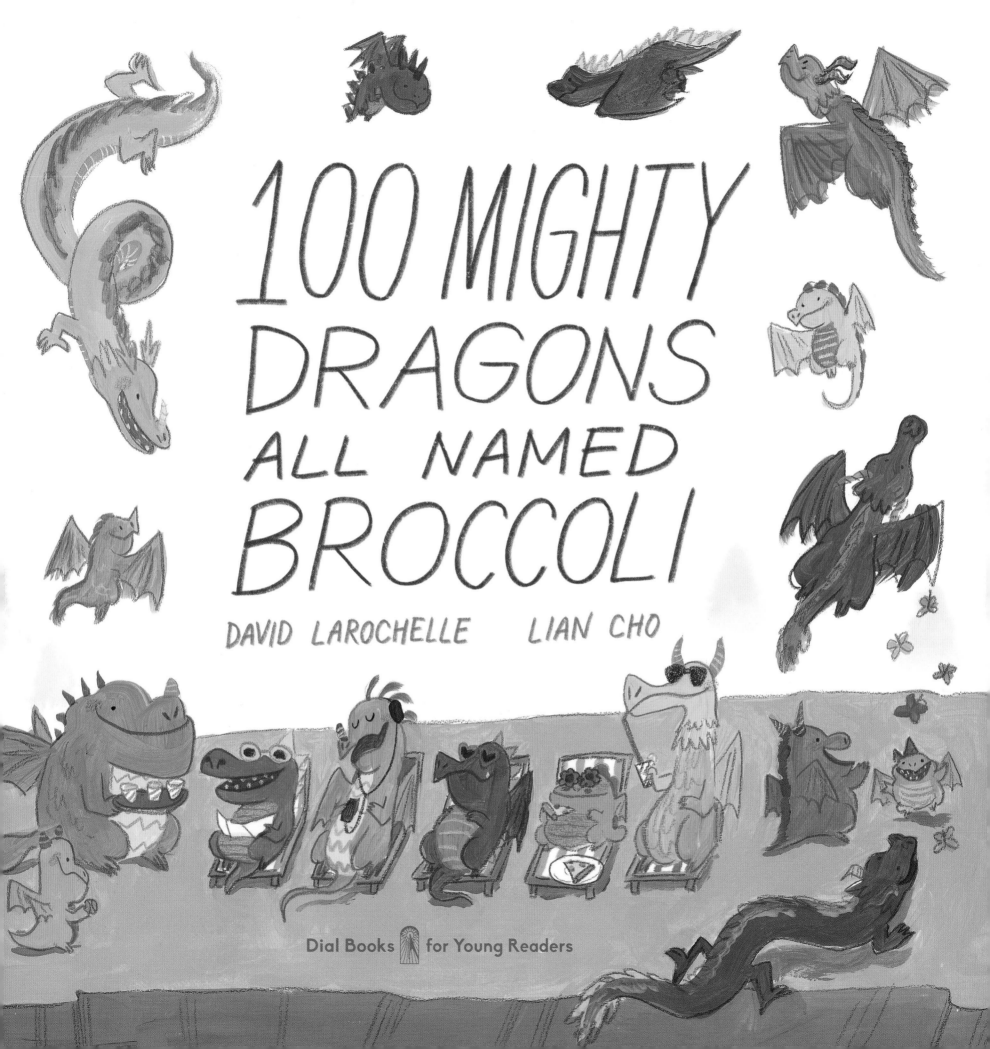

100 MIGHTY DRAGONS ALL NAMED BROCCOLI

DAVID LAROCHELLE   LIAN CHO

Dial Books for Young Readers

High on a mountain near a deep dark cave lived

100 mighty dragons.

They were all named Broccoli.

One blustery autumn day a tremendous
wind blew half the dragons away.

This left . . .

50 mighty dragons, all named Broccoli.

10 dragons sailed away on a cruise ship and became professional surfers in Hawaii.

This left . . .

40 mighty dragons, all named Broccoli.

The oldest dragon and the youngest dragon took a train to New York City and started their own heavy metal band.

This left . . .

38

mighty dragons all named Broccoli.

A mysterious wizard appeared and turned

1 dragon into a unicorn,

1 dragon into a werewolf

1 dragon into a zombie

and **1** dragon into a tiny pink poodle.

This left . . .

34 mighty dragons, all named Broccoli.

3 dragons moved to South Dakota.

3 dragons moved to North Carolina.

3 dragons moved to West Virginia.

3 dragons moved to East Texas.

This left . . .

22 mighty dragons, all named Broccoli.

All the dragons wearing sunglasses flew to France.

This left . . .

13 mighty dragons, all named Broccoli.

All the dragons wearing ballerina tutus flew to Sweden.   **This left . . .**

13 mighty dragons, all named Broccoli.

5

dragons took
a rocket to
the moon.

2

of the dragons from
West Virginia returned.

6 dragons moved to Hollywood and became famous movie stars.

The tiny pink poodle turned back into a dragon again.

And **3** dragons boarded a bus to Wisconsin to play football for the Green Bay Packers.

This left . . .

2 mighty dragons, both named Broccoli.

Another tremendous wind came along
and blew half the dragons away.

This left . . .

1 mighty dragon named Broccoli, all alone, high on a mountain near a deep dark cave.

One lonely dragon named Broccoli looked at the gray autumn sky. She crawled into the cave and disappeared.

This left . . .

O mighty dragons named Broccoli.

Winter came

and winter passed.

When spring finally arrived, Broccoli emerged from her cave and smiled a mighty grin.

She was followed by . . .

Mabel

Bob

Anika

Tyrone

Ruby

Emerald

Elvis

Maria

Twinkletoes

Frank

Hank

Lateesha

Hot Potato

Malik

Mateo

Duke

Sassafras

Poindexter

Peter

Paul

Mary

Azra

Frankie

Johnny

Toshi

And she knew exactly what to name them:

Sam · Little Joe · Hornet · Bubblegum-breath · Buster

Gumdrop · Ishmael · Mario · Luigi · Jackson

Sonny Boy · Frodo · Lassie · Lucas · Harley

Kumquat · Sasha · Tulip · Tex · Aliyah

Cucumber · Carrot · Fireball · Hans · Yoshiro

Dan

Stan

Fran

Microwave Oven

Ying

Abdul

Elizabeth

BeeBee

Tom

Tim

Ashley

Gomez

Mr. Chutney

Makalya

Sweetie Pie

Izzy

Min-ji

Marcos

Fifi

Zola

Zora

Zippy

Zev

Ahmed

Bongo-Billy

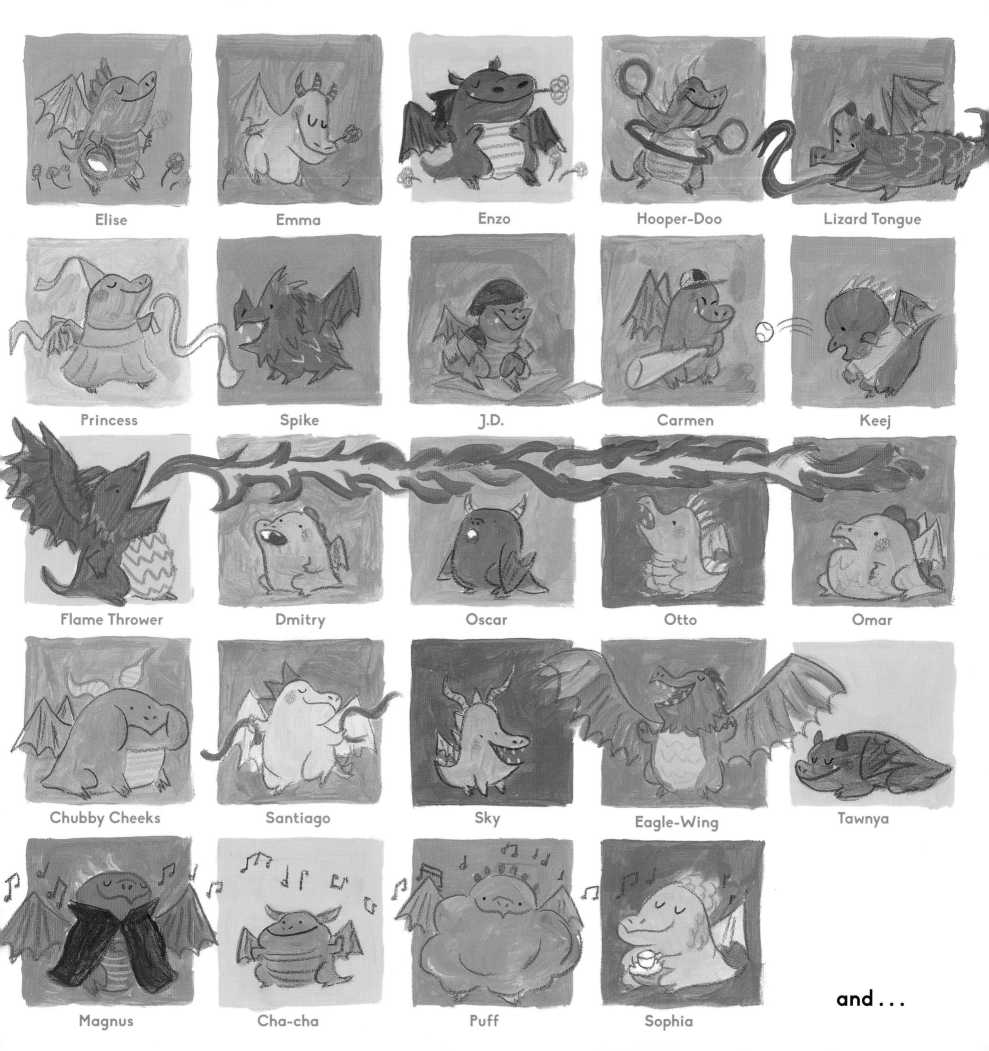

Elise

Emma

Enzo

Hooper-Doo

Lizard Tongue

Princess

Spike

J.D.

Carmen

Keej

Flame Thrower

Dmitry

Oscar

Otto

Omar

Chubby Cheeks

Santiago

Sky

Eagle-Wing

Tawnya

Magnus

Cha-cha

Puff

Sophia

and . . .

BROCCOLI JUNIOR!